Clifford THE BIG RED DOG
Thanksgiving Parade

by Maria S. Barbo
Illustrated by Artful Doodlers

Based on the Scholastic book series
"Clifford The Big Red Dog"
by Norman Bridwell

ISBN 978-0-545-25332-1

Designed by Michael Massen

12   11   10   9   8   7   6   5   4   3   2   10   11   12   13   14/0

Printed in the U.S.A.   40
First printing, October 2010

SCHOLASTIC INC.

New York   Toronto   London   Auckland
Sydney   Mexico City   New Delhi   Hong Kong

Clifford the Big Red Dog loved holidays.

He loved Thanksgiving best of all.

Clifford gave thanks for many things.

Clifford gave thanks for his little blue wagon.

Clifford gave thanks for his big red

doghouse.

Clifford was thankful for big piles of leaves to jump in.

"Woof!" Clifford barked.

He was thankful for big hills to roll down.

"Whee!" Clifford said.

Most of all, Clifford was thankful for
friends and family.

He loved Emily Elizabeth.

She helped make a big Thanksgiving dinner every year.

YUM!

Looking at all of the food was making
Clifford hungry!

His tummy growled.

Rumble. Rumble.

Clifford and his friends tried not to think about food.

It was hard.

But Mac had an idea.

"Let's go to the parade!" he said.

The Thanksgiving Day parade was fun.

The whole town went to cheer.

Clifford liked the parade.

But his tummy growled.

Rumble. Rumble.

"It's time for dinner!" called Emily
Elizabeth.

The friends all cheered.

Clifford could not wait to eat a turkey dinner.

But something was wrong.

The table was broken.

Dinner had fallen on the floor.

They could not eat the turkey.

They had no corn or green beans.

The stuffing was a mess!

Emily Elizabeth looked like she was going

to cry.

Clifford and his friends were sad.

T-Bone howled, *"A-rooo!"*

Then Cleo had an idea.

"There is corn at my house!" she said.

T-Bone jumped up and down. "There's stuffing at mine!"

"We can save dinner!" Mac said.

Cleo hopped home.

T-Bone and Mac raced.

Clifford had a thought.

We need a turkey!

Clifford ran to town as fast as he could.

He jumped over a big pile of leaves.

He rolled down a great big hill.

Big red dogs are very fast.

Ding-dong!

The doorbell rang at Clifford's house.

Emily Elizabeth went to the door.

"Surprise!"

Cleo and Mrs. Diller held a bowl of corn.

T-Bone and Sheriff Lewis had stuffing.

Jetta and Mac made green beans.

Clifford had the biggest surprise of all. A turkey!

"I am so thankful!" said Emily Elizabeth.

Clifford and his friends ate turkey.

They all had a good time together.

Clifford gave thanks for friends and family.
He was thankful for yummy food and a
warm home.

But most of all, Clifford was thankful to be
a big red dog.

Because big red dogs give great big hugs!

Do You Remember?

Circle the right answer.

1. What was Clifford thankful for?
    a. Friends
    b. Family
    c. Friends and family

2. Who had the idea to go to the parade?
    a. Mac
    b. Clifford
    c. T-Bone

Which happened first?

Which happened next?

Which happened last?

Write a 1, 2, or 3 in the space after each sentence.

Clifford ate a turkey dinner. _____

Clifford jumped in a big pile of leaves. _____

Clifford went to the parade. _____

Answers: